For Lowen, my worry-busting best b

Little Bean

www.littlebeanpublishing.co.uk
First published in the UK in 2018 by Little Bean Publishing Ltd.

Printed and bound in the UK by Dartprint, Tavistock.
ISBN 978 1 912512 00 3

It was very, very early in the morning.
So early, that the birds had not even woken up yet.

But Tom was awake. He was awake because he had a worry going around and around inside his head.

Suddenly, a shadowy superhero-shaped figure appeared at the window.

"LET ME IN!" the figure bellowed. "MY WORRY DETECTOR IS GOING BESERK OUT HERE. YOU NEED MY HELP!"

"Who are you?" asked Tom as he tentatively opened the window.

"CAPTAIN WORRYBUSTER AT YOUR SERVICE!" shouted the superhero as he climbed in.

"Oh, nice to meet you," said Tom, politely holding out his hand.

"FIST BUMP!" shouted the Captain. They bumped fists.

"Do you have to be quite so loud?" asked Tom. "It's very early."

"No problem!" said the Captain. "I'll turn it down a bit."
His voice was still pretty loud. "So, do you want to tell me what
you are worrying about? The reading on my worry detector is
off the scale."

"Not really," said Tom. "What's a worry detector?"

"I'll show you," said the Captain. "HOLD ON TIGHT!
WE'RE GOING WORRY-BUSTING!"

"Umm... I'm not supposed to go anywhere with strangers,"
said Tom.

"I'M A SUPERHERO!" shouted the Captain. "YOU'LL BE SAFE
WITH ME. AND WE'LL BE BACK BEFORE YOUR PARENTS
EVEN WAKE UP!"

They flew high above the town, and then even higher so Tom could see other towns and cities dotted across the landscape. The Captain held out his worry detector and the needle jumped up and down all over the place.

"Look!" he said. "Lots of people down there are worrying about something right now. That little girl has got a worry going around in her head too. She should be asleep. It's not much fun worrying, is it?"

"No," said Tom. "Why do people worry?"

"I'LL SHOW YOU," shouted the Captain. "HOLD ON TIGHT, WE'RE GOING BACK IN TIME!"

They flew super fast, backwards around the world.

"I feel a bit sick," said Tom.

"Ah, yes," said the Captain. "Time travel always does that. NEARLY THERE!"

With a slight jolt, they arrived at the edge of a forest, a million years in the past.

"Wow!" said Tom, looking at the enormous prehistoric trees. He reached out and touched a strange, spiky leaf.

"Look," whispered the Captain. There was a group of cavemen sitting around a fire. "They are all worrying too."

"What have they got to worry about?" asked Tom.

"They worry about the dangers in the woods. They worry about finding food to eat. And they worry about getting separated from each other and lost. All those worries keep them safe and help them survive."

"Your world in the future is much safer, Tom. And you have people looking after you and keeping you safe. But your brain is worrying like a caveman's brain. If there isn't something dangerous for it to worry about, it worries about lots of other stuff instead."

"Oh!" said Tom. "So it's just my brain being a bit silly?"

"Well, yes," said the Captain. "You don't need to worry about all those things. You're not a caveman, are you?"

"I suppose not!" said Tom with a smile. "But how do I stop worrying so much?"

"I know something that may help you," said the Captain. "HOLD ON TIGHT!"

This time they flew forward in time, super fast, all the way to ancient Greece. They landed by a large stone building just as the sun was rising over the sea. A girl was sitting on the rocks, looking out over the water.

"Captain WorryBuster!" she called out when she saw them. They bumped fists.

"Akilina, this is Tom," said the Captain. "I thought you might have something to help Tom with his worries."

"I do." She smiled and reached into her pocket. She took out a small stone and put it into Tom's hand. It felt smooth and had a dent in the middle where his thumb fitted nicely.

"What is it?" asked Tom.

"It's a worry stone," said Akilina. "Just rub it when you feel worried and you might find it helps you feel better."

"Thank you," said Tom. "I'll try that."

"RIGHT!" shouted the Captain. "HOLD ON TIGHT! TIME TO GO HOME!"

They flew super fast above the clouds this time and Tom could see vast blue oceans down below.

"I'll tell you a secret," said the Captain, "Once, I was afraid of heights."

Tom laughed at the thought of this, as they probably couldn't be flying any higher. He could even see the stars and a satellite.

"I used to worry about falling out of the sky if I went too high," the Captain continued, "but I didn't want to be a superhero that just flew along the ground. So, I set myself the challenge of going a little higher each day. And you know what?"

"What?" asked Tom.

"In the end I did it! Sometimes you just have to face your fears and keep trying. And falling out of the sky isn't half as scary as I thought. I've done it LOADS of times now," the Captain said with a grin. "We're nearly back at your house now."

Tom felt quite relieved that they hadn't fallen out of the sky today.

They climbed back in through the window of Tom's bedroom.

"WILL YOU LOOK AT THAT!" shouted the Captain, holding up his worry detector. "THERE IS NOTHING LIKE A BIT OF FRESH AIR AND ADVENTURE TO HELP BLOW THE WORRIES AWAY."

"Yes," said Tom, "I do feel better. But can you be a bit quieter please? My parents are still asleep."

"Okay!" said the Captain, still quite loudly. He really was quite a shouty superhero.

"So, next time you are feeling worried," said the Captain, "try to get out of the house and do something with your friends or family. Go to the park or ride your bike. It will help take your mind off your worries. And remember to use your worry stone!"

"Okay," said Tom, "I'll try that. Thank you."

"And one last thing," said the Captain. "Sometimes it really helps to tell someone what you are worried about. Someone in your family, a teacher or a friend."

"Okay," said Tom. "But it doesn't seem like such a big worry anymore. Can I tell you?"

"OF COURSE!" shouted the Captain.

Tom reached up and whispered his worry into the Captain's ear. The Captain smiled and nodded, and Tom smiled too.

"FIST BUMP!" they both shouted and bumped fists.

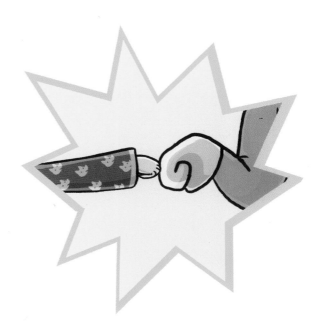

The Captain climbed out of the window and flew off into the distance.

Tom slipped back into bed and snuggled down under the covers. He really did feel much better after his adventure, but he was tired out from all the travelling.

Tom held the worry stone tightly in his hand. It was still very, very early, and soon he was fast asleep.

www.captainworrybuster.co.uk